WRITTEN AND
TYLER

MW00340531

THE ADVENTURES OF
GRANDPA JACK

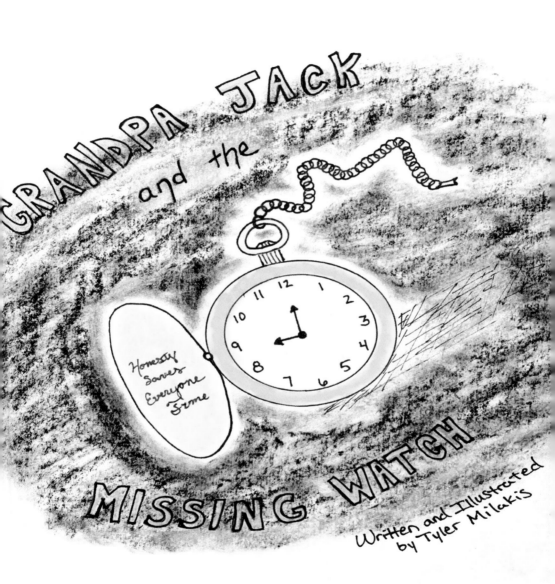

GRANDPA JACK and the

MISSING WATCH

Honesty Saves Everyone Time

Written and Illustrated by Tyler Milakis

1

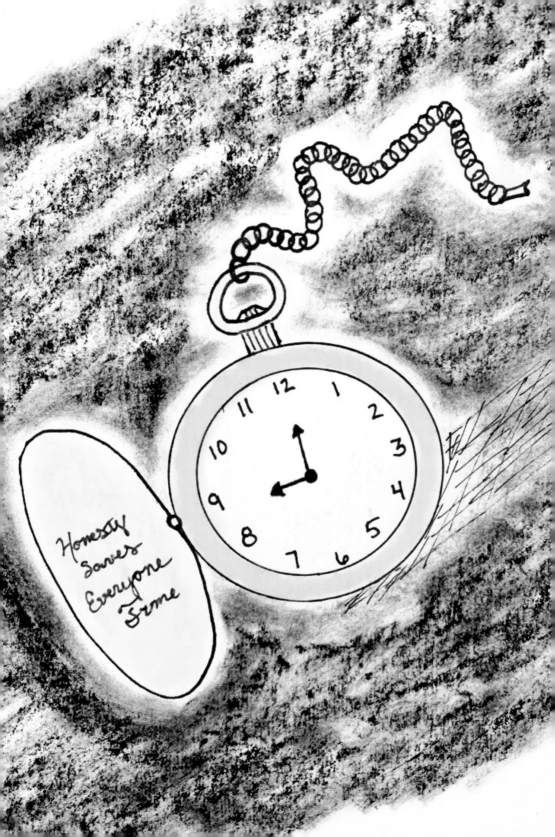

Grandpa Jack was a very sentimental man, meaning he loved items that have been passed down from generation to generation. These special items meant something to him. One of these items was a pocket watch that belonged to his great-grandfather. It was gold, and shiny, with a few scratches on it that told the story of its journey. Those scratches on it gave the watch character, and made it even more special. Inside the front cover of the pocket watch was a saying that was engraved on it. It said, "Honesty Saves Everyone Time."

One day, Jasper and his little cousin, Isaac, were over at Grandpa Jack's. These two knew the rules and were a big help to Grandpa Jack. However, this day they had company. Aunt Linda had dropped off her two twin boys, Frederick and Charles. These two did NOT play by the rules, and were like two bulls in a china shop. They bumped, and they clanked, and they galloped through the house as if it were an indoor playground.

Today's big chore was to give the dogs a bath. Grandpa Jack had two dachshunds, and all of the grandkids always laughed when they saw the dogs because they looked like two hot dogs with four little legs.

"OK, Jasper and Isaac, you two help me with Wrinkles first. Frederick and Charles, can I trust you to watch Wrigley until the first bath is done?"

"Yessss, Grandpaaa Jacckkk."
the twins said suspiciously at the
same time.

Grandpa Jack pushed up his sleeves,
set his pocket watch on his bedside
table, and proceeded into the
bathroom to give Wrinkles his bath.

Wrigley looked at Frederick and Charles and knew that no good would come from being around them and ran off to the other room to hide. They chased him around the house. Wrigley was quick and knew all the best hiding spots! Suddenly…the two boys stopped chasing the dog. That's when they noticed it!

Beaming out of the corner of their eyes was the golden pocket watch.

It was as if the watch was whispering the boys' names…*Frederick…. Charles….take me!*

The two boys took it and ran downstairs.

Grandpa Jack noticed that Wrigley was hiding underneath the bed, no twin boys to be found anywhere. He simply shook his head and plopped Wrigley into the bathtub to finish the chore with Jasper and Isaac. Once they were done, Grandpa Jack noticed that the two twin boys weren't the only thing that had disappeared. He noticed his watch had gone missing!

"Frederick! Charles! Can I see you in my room, please!"

There was silence. Not a peep from the two boys.

"Boys! Now!" Grandpa Jack repeated.

"Uh oh! We're busted!" whispered Frederick.

"Not a peep, Frederick! Maybe he doesn't know!" Charles whispered back.

"Yessss, Grandpaaa Jackkkk?" the two boys asked.

Grandpa Jack already knew the answer to his question, but he asked it anyway. "Have you two seen my pocket watch that was on the bedside table? It seems to be missing."

Charles spoke first, "Noooo, Grandpa Jack. No watch here. Haven't seen it. Couldn't even tell you what it looked like."

"What are you talking about Charles? You know what it looks like. It's the gold one in your back pock- uh....I mean....Noooo, we haven't seen it!" Frederick fumbled trying to correct his story.

"Frederick! You knucklehead! You just told him!" Charles shouted.

Defeated, Charles pulled the pocket watch

out of his back pocket and handed it over. Grandpa Jack sat both of the boys down. Knowing they were caught in a lie, they started to cry.

"Now, boys. It's one thing to take something from someone else – which is wrong, but it's another thing to lie about it – which is really wrong." Grandpa Jack spoke in a soft voice.

"Charles, can you read the inside cover of the watch for me?" Grandpa Jack asked.

"I guess so. It says, "Honesty Saves Everyone Time." What does that mean?" Charles asked.

It all started when Harrison and his little cousin, Owen, came over to Grandpa Jacks house for game night. No one saw it coming….no one knew what to do…except, Grandpa Jack. Let's back up a little bit, here. It was Sunday night, and it was game night! It was a tradition that Grandpa Jack started with Harrison when Harrison was only five-years-old. Owen had just turned five, as well, and Harrison thought it was time to bring the tradition to his other cousins.

The games would vary depending on what new games they got and what mood they were in. Tonight, they were playing connect-four, a game where you had to get four checkers in a row by putting them into these little slots. Grandpa was really good, and Harrison wasn't too bad either. However, Owen was still learning, and his skills weren't quite there yet. Harrison played Grandpa Jack first, and won.

Grandpa Jack wanted a rematch, but he was no match for Harrison, and accepted defeat again.

"It's my turn!" shouted Owen.

"OK, buddy, you can play against me since Grandpa Jack lost." replied Harrison.

The game started, and Harrison tried to go easy on Owen at first.

Then, Owen put his checker in a spot that easily allowed Harrison to win. Without hesitation, Harrison put his red checker into the winning slot. Owen silently stared at the game, starting to realize that he lost. Tears started to well up in Owen's eyes, and without warning, took the game and threw it up in the air. Black and red checkers rained down from the sky.

"I hate this game! I can't do anything! I want to go home!" Owen screamed out.

Owen then ran out of the room. Harrison and Grandpa Jack looked at each other with the "what just happened?" look in their eyes.

"Looks like it's time for a talk." Grandpa Jack said as he got out of his chair.

Grandpa Jack found Owen hiding under the kitchen table, with Owen's feet peeking out from under the table cloth. Grandpa Jack climbed under the table with Owen.

"Hey bud, what was that all about?"
Grandpa Jack asked, trying to
console Owen.

"I can't help it! I get so mad and then
so sad. It happens so fast that I can't
stop it!" Owen cried out.

"Well, that's just your super
power coming out." Grandpa
Jack reassured.

"Super power?" Owen asked, wiping
away tears off his face.

"Yeah! You have the super power of big, big feelings!" Grandpa said with a smile on his face. "A lot of people can only experience one emotion at a time, and a lot of those people don't even know how to handle THAT emotion! You don't hold back on your emotions, and when you "feel" something…you "feel it" BIG! But just like any super hero, it takes time to master control over your super power."

"Like how the Hulk broke a lot of things at first, but then learned how to control his strength?" Owen asked, starting to lighten up.

"Haha, exactly like the Hulk! So, how can we help find a way for you to master this new super power?"

"Maybe, when I start to feel the big feelings come up, I can take a deep breath, and walk away for a second. That's what the Hulk does." Owen said.

"I think that's perfect! Back when Grandpa Jack was in the Navy, if we were frustrated or scared, we would take a deep breath in for four seconds, and then breath out for four seconds. Let's try it." Grandpa Jack suggested.

After a few moments of practicing breathing, Owen was calm. They climbed out from underneath the kitchen table. With a big smile, and tears dried, Owen gave his grandpa a hug.

"Thanks, Grandpa Jack! We make a great team, because I think that your super power is the power to calm people down!" Owen mentioned.

"Thanks, buddy! After all, super powers run in the family!" Grandpa Jack said with a wink.

THE END

GRANDPA JACK and the

MAGIC SMILE

Written and Illustrated by
Tyler Milakis

"Guys! Grandpa Jack can do magic! It's amazing!" Harrison shouted to his brothers, Joey and Nico.

"What do you mean, magic?" asked Nico.

"OK, so here's what happened…"

Harrison started to tell the story.

It was a Saturday morning, and the first day of 5th grade was on Monday. Grandpa Jack offered to take Harrison school supply shopping, and to get new shoes for school.

When they got to the mall parking lot, there was one last parking spot left. Grandpa Jack put on his turn signal for the spot, but another car tried to go for the same spot. This lady looked mean, and a bit crazy! Grandpa Jack smiled his biggest smile, and then the lady smiled back and waved Grandpa Jack to take the spot. That's when Harrison noticed something going on.

They got to the school supply store, and went through the list and got every item they needed to bring to class. They started to get in line, but the store was packed with back-to-school shoppers. Grandpa Jack and Harrison waited patiently in line, while everyone else around them started to get restless. One of the employees saw the line, and then made eye contact with Grandpa Jack, as he smiled his biggest smile.

The employee came up and whispered, "I can check you out over here." pointing to an open checkout counter.

"Oh, well thank you!" Grandpa Jack politely said.

Harrison noticed this happen twice now. Curiosity took over, and he had to ask what was going on!

"OK, spill the beans. How are you doing that? How are you getting this amazing treatment from complete strangers?!" Harrison demanded.

With a chuckle, Grandpa Jack replied, "Well, it's kind of like magic. A lot of people are stressed, and expect other people to be rude. But, if you smile at them and let them know that you see them and act polite and happy, then maybe…just maybe…some of that happiness will rub off and some stress with fall away."

"Does it work all the time?" Harrison asked.

"Not always, but I'd rather share a free smile with someone anyways." Grandpa Jack said.

The next stop was the shoe store. They got to the crowded store, and Harrison found the perfect pair of shoes to show off on the first day of school. They were white with black and blue stripes along the side. Chuck, the neighborhood bully, saw the same pair of shoes. It just so happened that Chuck and Harrison both wore the same shoe size.

The salesman came out with only one shoebox. Harrison and Chuck both reached for the box.

"Sorry, fellas. We only have one pair of shoes left in that size." the salesman mentioned.

Expecting to get punched in the face if Harrison tried to take the shoes away from Chuck, he remembered the magic trick that Grandpa Jack had been doing all day. He looked Chuck right in the eyes, and smiled his biggest smile.

"It's fine, Chuck can have them." Harrison said proudly.

Without warning, something completely unexpected happened next.

"Nah, you can have them, Harrison. I'll look for another pair. See ya around!" Chuck said with a smile on his face.

Grandpa Jack noticed what had just happened. He crossed his arms proudly, and purchased the pair of shoes for Harrison.

As they left the store, Grandpa Jack whispered, "Nicely done, Ol' Sport!"

After telling the story to his brothers, all of the boys were ready to share this magic trick with everyone at school! They would all walk in smiling their biggest smiles!

THE END

GRANDPA JACK BECOMES...

Howdy Doo!

A DINOSAUR

Written and Illustrated by Tyler Milakis

It's no surprise that Grandpa Jack and his family have big imaginations! That's why they take the best road trips, build the best forts, and have the most fun! Isaac was always known for having one of the biggest imaginations in the family. But then Owen came along. He took having a big imagination to the next level!

Owen was obsessed with dinosaurs! He even created an imaginary friend who was a big, green tyrannosaurus rex named, Marvin, to help keep the monsters away when he was asleep in the dark. After all, what monster would mess with a big, green t-rex!?

Owen and Isaac came over for a sleep over and movie night at Grandpa Jacks. The two young boys would often compete for who was more creative and more imaginative. As the boys unpacked their overnight bags, they came up with ideas.

"We could pretend like we're in a castle, and a dragon got loose, and it's up to us to stop it! We could make armor out of cardboard and even have swords, too!" suggested Isaac.

"Or, we could pretend like we have super powers. I could freeze stuff with my mind, and you can move objects with your mind. I even have blue pajamas so it's like I'm made of ice. We can get string and tie to stuff and move it like you're controlling it with your mind!" Owen countered.

Isaac knew that his cousin's imagination was slightly better than his!

"OK...I actually love that idea!" Isaac said, admitting defeat.

The boys went to go unpack.

"OH, NO!!!! My t-rex dinosaur toy! It's not here! I can't sleep without it!" Owen cried out.

Grandpa Jack happened to be walking by and overheard Owen's dilemma.

"Boys, why don't you go play, and I'll keep looking for your dinosaur." Grandpa said.

"OK, his name is Marvin, grandpa. He's my protector against monsters and bad guys! I wish he was real and could be with me always!" Owen said sadly.

"Well, you never know…sometimes wishes can come true! Now, go play while I get you two unpacked." Grandpa Jack said as he sent the boys off.

Grandpa Jack went into the attic, and found an old Halloween box. He opened it up, hoping to find what he was looking for.

"Ah, ha!" Grandpa Jack said, relieved. "Here it is!" Grandpa Jack grabbed a night light from the old box, and then filled up a squirt bottle with lavender-scented water, as well.

The boys played for hours and hours, constantly adding new ideas to their play time. They ate pizza, which became a feast fit for a king. They watched movies, which became a drive-in movie theater. They took their bath, which became a fight for survival after their ship had sunk. Finally, it was time for bed.

"Did you find Marvin?" Owen asked Grandpa Jack after he was all tucked in.

"No, buddy, I didn't. But if you believe hard enough, then Marvin will still protect you even if you don't have your toy. Use that imagination of yours." Grandpa Jack said as he flipped off the light switch.

Without Marvin, Owen heard every CREAK…every BUMP…and every SCRATCH. He yelled out, "MONSTERS!"

Then, the door opened. In the doorway was the shadow of what could only be a big, green tyrannosaurus rex! Grandpa Jack, having a big imagination himself, had found and old dinosaur costume from a few Halloweens ago, and thought it could help.

"Marvin!? Is that you!?" Owen said as he sat up.

"Hi Owen! It is! It's Marvin! I heard you had some monsters in the room, and I came to help." Grandpa Jack said.

"How are you here!? I thought I lost you!" Owen asked.

"If you believe hard enough, anything is possible! I have some things that might be able to help. I have this squirt bottle with magical water that keeps monsters away, and I'm letting you have my special t-rex night light, too!" Grandpa Jack reassured.

"Thanks, Marvin! I can finally go to sleep without worrying about the monsters getting me! Owen laid back down, waving goodbye to his t-rex friend as the door closed.

The next morning, Isaac, Owen, and Grandpa Jack were all having breakfast.

"So, how did you boys sleep?" Grandpa Jack asked with a smirk on his face.

"Good." Isaac said.

"Well, I slept great last night! Marvin came by and gave me monster spray and this really cool night light! I don't think I'll need him to come by as much anymore since the night light was *his* special night light, and it keeps *all* the monsters away!" Owen said.

"Wow! That's incredible, buddy! Marvin, sounds like a great friend!" Grandpa Jack said.

Owen finished with, "He is grandpa! He actually reminds me of you a lot!"

THE END

GRANDPA JACK and ONE, CRAZY FAMILY

Written & Illustrated by Tyler Milakis

The holidays were chaotic at Grandpa Jack's house. The *whole* family came over! They would eat and laugh, and sing Christmas songs, and read Christmas stories. It was the perfect time to bring the whole family together, embrace family traditions, and catch up on what was going on in everyone's life.

Grandpa Jack especially loved having everyone at his home…Isabella and her sons, Harrison, Nico, and Joey, Aunt Shirley and Uncle Thomas with their kids Jasper, Owen, Ashley, and Olivia, Uncle Frank and Aunt Beverly and their kids James, and Christine, Aunt Genevieve, Aunt Linda and Uncle Carl with their twin boys Frederick and Charles, and Aunt Priscilla with her three kids, Isaac, Greg, and Tabitha.

They had dinner and dinner got very loud in this family! The kids would secretly try to throw food at each other, and Isaac would always feed the dogs under the table. All of the uncles would talk about who they thought was going to win the big game coming up, while all of the aunts gossiped about the latest news in the neighborhood. Grandpa Jack and Grandma Louise would sit at the end of the table, and just take it all in.

Grandpa Jack was the kind of person who never needed to talk at the dinner table. He would just smile and look around at his amazing family, casually sipping his iced tea. Grandpa Jack looked across the table to his wife, and smiled the biggest smile ever! Grandma Louise knew what that smile meant…that he wouldn't want to be anywhere else on earth!

Harrison stood up and started to tap his glass of milk with a spoon.

CLING! CLING! CLING!

"Excuse me, everyone. I'd like to make a toast. Now, I know it's Christmas Eve and we're excited about getting to open one present tonight, but I wanted to say a few things. I know we don't always get along, or say the right things, but at the end of the day — we show up for each other. We come together as a family, and practice how to be the best versions of ourselves that we can be. And I want to say thank you to Grandpa Jack for being the best teacher of so many lessons over the years. You hold this family together, and inspire us to be our best versions. Merry Christmas, everyone!"

As the night progressed, it was time to read Twas the Night Before Christmas. It was a family tradition. As they got half way through the book, they heard a knock on the window. Everyone was shocked when they opened the door.

"IT'S SANTA!!!" screamed Isaac.

"Ho, Ho, Ho!" Santa bellowed out loud.

"I hear we have a lot of good boys and girls here tonight, and I know it's early, but I just couldn't wait to stop by! I made a deal with Grandpa Jack, and we agreed that you get to open TWO presents tonight!" laughed Santa.

Santa, gave every aunt, uncle, grandkid, cousin, niece, and nephew one box wrapped in gold wrapping paper. As they all started to open the box, it was the same item in every single one…a picture frame with their family photo in it, and a note that said, *Family is Everything!*

As the kids looked up to ask Santa how he got a family picture of them all, he had disappeared.

As they stood in disbelief, Jasper stood up and broke the silence.

"I'd like to make a toast, here's to not only Christmas magic, but also to family, because family truly is everything!" Jasper spoke as he held up his lemonade.

They continued to open their presents. As Harrison finished opening his gifts, he looked around and then looked over to Grandpa Jack, smiled the biggest smile ever… letting his grandpa know that he wouldn't want to be anywhere else on earth!

THE END

VOCABULARY FROM THE TEXT

Book 1: Grandpa Jack and the Missing Watch

- sentimental (cen-te-ment-al) – feelings of tenderness and memories

- generation (jen-er-a-shun) – members of a family living at the same time

- galloped (gal-up-d) – to run fast and loud like that of a horse

- suspiciously (sus-pish-us-lee) – done with caution or distrust

- proceeded (pro-seed-ed) – to continue an activity that was paused

- plopped (pl-op-d) – to set down quickly in a clumsy way

- fumbled (fum-bl-d) – to lose control of something in your hands or words

VOCABULARY FROM THE TEXT

Book 2: Grandpa Jack and the Big, Big Feelings

- tradition (tr-uh-dish-un) – customs or beliefs passed down in a family

- accepted (ak-sep-ted) – believed to be correct or valid

- hesitation (hez-i-tay-shun) – to pause or wait before an action

- console (con-sol) – to comfort someone during a tough time

- reassured (re-ash-er-d) – to say or do something to remove fear or doubt

- experience (ex-peer-ee-ence) – to encounter an event or occurrence

- frustrated (fr-uh-sh-tr-ate-ed) – feeling distress because of not being able to do something

VOCABULARY FROM THE TEXT

Book 3: Grandpa Jack and the Magic Smile

- restless (rest-less) – unable to relax

- stressed (st-ress-d) – to feel mental or emotional tension

- crowded (cr-ow-d-ed) – a space full of people or objects

- neighborhood (nay-bor-hood) – an area with a community of people

- unexpected (un-ex-pec-ted) – not prepared for something to happen

VOCABULARY FROM THE TEXT

Book 4: Grandpa Jack Becomes a Dinosaur

- imaginations (i-mag-i-nay-shun) – to create new ideas or situations within one's mind

- obsessed (ob-sess-d) – intense focus or admiration for something

- controlling (con-troll-ing) – to remain in charge at all costs

- dilemma (dih-lem-ah) – a problem or tricky situation

- constantly (con-stan-t-lee) – without stopping or pause

VOCABULARY FROM THE TEXT

Book 5: Grandpa Jack and One, Crazy Family

- chaotic (kay-aw-tic) – without control or order

- secretly (see-cret-lee) – keeping something hidden from others

- gossiped (g-oss-ip-d) – to talk about someone without them knowing or being present

- progressed (pro-gr-ess-d) – to continue on a path that was already started

- bellowed (bell-oh-d) – to voice out loud or yell

ABOUT JACK

Jack H. Keen was an amazing grandfather, known for drinking iced tea on hot days, wearing pungent cologne, fedora hats, and fancy watches, known for his famous "Howdy Doo" greeting, and tickle extraordinaire.
He served in the U.S. Navy during World War II, and remained a true friend to his troopmates after the war. He loved dachshunds, his Grinch sweatshirt, and most importantly – family time!

ABOUT THE AUTHOR

Tyler Milakis is an educator, artist, author, wellness coach, and yoga teacher. His passion for being a "jack of all trades" comes from Grandpa Jack's hard work ethic. Tyler was born in Indianapolis, Indiana, attended Purdue University with a major in Art and Design, and currently resides in Denver, Colorado with his dachshund, Wrigley, but plans to move back to Chicago, IL. Tyler loves pungent cologne, fedora hats, fancy watches, but most importantly – family time!